The
BEAR UNDER THE STAIRS

story and pictures by Helen Cooper

SCHOLASTIC INC. New York   Toronto   London   Auckland   Sydney

For Ted

ISBN 0-590-48539-3

18 17 16 15   5 6 7 8/0

Printed in the U.S.A.   09

First Scholastic printing, May 1994

William was scared of grizzly bears,
and William was scared of the
place under the stairs.

It was all because
one day he thought
he saw a bear,
hiding there,
under the stairs.

And so he slammed the
door quick —
wham, bang, thump!

After that, William worried about the bear.
He wondered what it might eat.
"Yum, yum," he thought he heard the
bear whisper. "I'm a very hungry bear,
and maybe I'll eat a boy for lunch."

So William saved a pear for the bear
that lived there, under the stairs.

And when no one was watching,
William crept down the hall,
cracked open the door,
threw the pear to the bear
that lived under the stairs,
and slammed the door quick —
wham, bang, thump!

William had kept his eyes shut tight,
so he didn't actually see the bear
in its lair
under the stairs. . . .

But he knew what it looked like!

And at night

while William dreamed . . .

Every day William fed
the bear that lived
under the stairs.

He fed it bananas, bacon, and bread.

He fed it
hazelnuts,
haddock,
and honey.

But he always kept his eyes shut
tight, and slammed the door quick —
wham, bang, thump!

After a while there was a strange smell
in the air
near the bear
under the stairs.
The smell got stronger and stronger . . .

until William's mom noticed it.
"What's that awful smell!" she said.
"It seems to be coming
from there, under the stairs.
I think I'd better take a look."

"NO!"

shouted William, very scared.

"Don't go in there!"

"William, what's the matter?" Mom asked
as she lifted him onto her lap.
So William told her all about the hungry bear
in its lair, there, under the stairs.

Then William and Mom decided to scare
the bear that lived under the stairs.
William bravely kept his eyes wide open
this time,
and when they opened the door
he saw . . .

an old furry rug,
a broken chair,
and horrible stinky food everywhere . . .
but no scary bear!

So William and Mom
cleaned up the mess
under the stairs.

Then they went shopping and Mom
bought William a little brown grizzly
bear of his own. It had such a nice
face that William was never scared of bears . . .

or the place under the stairs, ever again.